Resolving Conflict Peacefully

MAZE OF THE FIRE DRAGON

TALES OF THE
EMPTY-HANDED MASTERS

by Terrence Webster-Doyle

Atrium Society Publications
Middlebury, Vermont

Distributed by North Atlantic Books
Berkeley, California

Atrium Publications
P.O. Box 816
Middlebury, VT 05753

First printing, 1992 Second printing, 1996

Illustrations: Rod Cameron
Cover Design: Robert Howard
Book Design, Editor: Charlene Koonce
Creative Consultant: Jean Webster-Doyle

Publisher's Cataloging in Publication Data
Prepared by Quality Books, Inc.

Webster-Doyle, Terrence, 1940–
Maze of the fire dragon : tales of the empty-handed masters / Terrence Webster-Doyle
p. cm.
SUMMARY: 20 stories set in a fictional martial arts training school, emphasizing the philosophical & spiritual aspects of the study of martial arts, such as non-violent conflict resolution, mental discipline, and the teacher-student relationship.

Audience: For ages 8–15
ISBN 0-942941-26-8 (pbk.)
ISBN 0-942941-27-6 (hbk.)

1. Martial arts – Juvenile fiction. I. Title. II. Title: Tales of the empty-handed masters.

PZ7.W4 1992 796.8
QBI92-312
Library of Congress Catalog Card Number: 92-070338

Atrium publications are available at special discounts for bulk purchases, premiums, fund-raising, or educational use. For details, contact:

Special Sales Director
Atrium Publications
P.O. Box 816
Middlebury, VT 05753
(800) 848-6021

Printed in Hong Kong

This book is dedicated to Martial Arts instructors of all styles and types. This is a book that goes beyond any one view and looks at the universal essence of all Martial Arts: understanding and resolving conflict peacefully. Our dedication as Martial Artists is to develop the tools and skills needed to live in harmony with other human beings; our dedication as educators is to bring these tools and skills to the children of the world. This is the challenge of education and the Martial Arts for the 21st Century.

Special thanks to all those people who are quoted herein. You have given us glimpses of the truth.

The foolish reject what they see,
Not what they think;
The wise reject what they think,
Not what they see.

— Huang Po

Dear Student,

Contained in this book are Tales from the Empty-Handed Masters, Martial Arts teachers who strived to educate their students to the true essence of the Martial Arts. These teachers knew that the Martial Arts help the student to develop not only physically but mentally — that regular practice contributes significantly to a healthier, happier life. These "Empty-Handed" (weaponless) masters transmitted their knowledge of self-defense skills with the understanding that the student will develop confidence and the ability *not* to fight! These teachers emphasized the importance of resolving conflict peacefully, and acting intelligently, so as not to create more violence in an already violent world. They were concerned that the Martial Arts be understood and experienced as a way to bring about peace, not — as many believe — to promote violence.

These tales are being passed on to you so that you can begin to understand what the masters of the Martial Arts mean when they say, "The Martial Arts promote peace and a healthy, happy life. They do not promote war!"

You may have to work hard to understand these stories. Working at understanding is similar to practicing a complicated physical form... It makes you stronger. And when you are stronger, you are less likely to fall into the trap of the Maze of the Fire Dragon.

You *can* do it!

Please note: I've written these "Tales of the Empty-Handed Masters" to explore ideas, feelings, and aspects of training which are common to *all* Martial Arts styles. My background is mainly in Japanese Karate, and I have used certain Japanese words such as *kiai*, *hara*, *hakama*, and *gi* — certainly not out of disrespect for other styles, but simply because they are the terms I am used to. You will see that these tales have universal significance and are meaningful to all Martial Artists, whatever their style.

Table of Contents

Tales of the Empty-Handed Masters

Waiting without expectation
The mind is still,
Open and unknowing.

The Puzzle

There was a young student who set out to study the Martial Arts. There was so much to learn that he became confused. He visited many schools and spoke with many teachers. One teacher stated, "This is the way, the *only* way!" Another teacher said, "This is the coveted path, the *true* style!" And on and on he went, through a maze of "ways" and "styles," looking for the real meaning of the Martial Arts.

Where can I turn? Who is telling me the truth? What is the true meaning of the Martial Arts? How do I find out? Questions plagued the student; he had to find an answer. He traveled far to reach a great master that the other teachers spoke of with respect. When the student arrived, he was granted permission to enter and speak with the revered master.

"Teacher, I am confused. I know that there is a deep truth within the Martial Arts, something much more important than simply learning self-defense skills. But I don't know who to trust. Everyone tells me something different, and each says that their way is the right way to follow. What shall I do?"

"Do you *really* want to find out, student? Or are you merely curious? If you are serious, then you must undergo a great and challenging adventure. You may not be successful; there is no guarantee. And at the end is the great unknown, the void from which you came! Are you willing to risk everything?" The old teacher looked at the student intently, with shining bright eyes.

"Yes, teacher. I am serious. I feel it deeply. I must know the essence of the Martial Arts."

"Then you must enter the Maze of the Fire Dragon! I will give you a puzzle to solve. Do so and you will be on your way to truly understanding the Martial Arts." The old man spoke with dignity and conviction.

"Here is the puzzle… You are caught in a maze of never-ending passages. Behind and gaining on you is a Fire Dragon! In front of you, down dark passages, are unknown dangers. It is certain that you will be burnt up by the Fire Dragon coming from behind if you cannot escape. So, what can you do to avoid being devoured? Solve this puzzle and you will understand the most powerful force in all Martial Arts training. You must escape from the Fire Dragon's maze — or perish… but don't worry too much! I have been through it myself and am here to help guide you. But no one can do it for you. It is up to you alone. Are you ready?"

Finding the real meaning of the Martial Arts is like looking for the glasses that are sitting on your nose.

— Anonymous

To See Before It is Seen

The graveyard was barely lit by a quarter moon. An owl hooted, then flew out of its hiding place, swooping down among the trees beyond. The night was still. He could feel his heart beating in his throat. This was a test of fear.

The other students had vanished. Each one had been told by the head instructor to spend time alone in the graveyard. He could feel the hairs standing up on the back of his neck.

Don't let your thoughts run wild. See how they try to frighten you. We have talked about death before. Death is the unknown. What you fear is the known, your images of death — not the fact of death! He remembered his teacher's words at their last meeting. They had discussed death — the death of the body and of the self, the self which is made up of a collection of thoughts that create "me." But tonight, what had seemed so clear was no longer clear. The student felt alone, overwhelmed by the reality of the graveyard.

He was surrounded by monuments to death: stone blocks with names, dates and last words. The presence of the dead around him, the silence, the eternal end to being alive, appeared as a black fathomless hole. He would catch his spinning thoughts as they began to whirl away into fantasies of ghosts of death. He shivered. Again and again he struggled to focus on what was real, and free himself from fantasy.

Even though the autumn night was warm, he was cold to his bones. The trees took on human-like forms. The owl hooted again and suddenly swooped down from the dark — large wings of prey descending on an unsuspecting nocturnal creature. He could smell the dampness in the soft soil under his feet. The

tombstones, eternal monuments to times gone forever, reminded him that there would be an end to all that he knew. He broke out in a cold sweat. An emptiness that no answer could fill overwhelmed him. This was the void, that abyss that all people fear. He was standing in it! He imagined that the dead were pulling him through the earth, ghost hands coming up through the ground, grasping his legs, pulling him down. His body was wet; his eyes ached from trying to see into the night. He was ready to complete this test!

A shadow passed across his vision; the student instinctively went into combat ready stance! Was it real, or a ghost? His heart pumped faster and his muscles tensed. Whatever it was, he was prepared!

Can you tell the difference between what is really there and what you think or imagine is there? Can you recognize an intention to hurt you even before the attacker feels it in himself or herself? This is the ability to be aware of what is going to happen, perhaps only a split second before it does happen. It is one of the finely-tuned skills of a master Martial Artist. With this ability, the Martial Artist can end the potential for harm — before any harm can occur. These clear, strong words of his teacher rang in his mind.

The shadow took form. A dark, massive figure emerged from behind the largest tombstone. It rose up out of the ground to a terrible height, towering in the black sky. The partial light from the quarter moon cast a dim eerie shadow across the ground toward the student. The student's body was frozen in combat stance! His legs were concrete and his eyes were fixed in terror on that hulk of a figure.

The student felt a scream emerging from deep down in his gut… It rose up to his throat, but stopped there, and only continued on as a thought in his brain. He watched every detail of the ghost-like figure, waiting for any sign of intended harm. The student's mind suddenly went blank. And as a wave subsides back into the ocean, the overpowering fear of that first moment of encounter subsided. There was only a heightened sense of awareness. It was as if time and the world stood absolutely still.

"What are you doing here?" rumbled an old deep voice from this great statue of death.

"Who are you that is asking?" he heard himself reply, surprised at the command and calm in his voice. It was as if the frightened boy had disappeared — and in his place a confident Martial Artist came forth. The dark figure before him began to take on more human dimensions and lost its superhuman presence. The figure was wearing a black jacket and a large hat that prevented the student from seeing who he might be.

"And who are you?" the deep voice bellowed. The figure seemed to grow taller with this commanding question. The student knew what was being asked.

"I am fear; there is only fear!" the student responded with confidence.

"Do you know what death is?" the large figure's voice boomed forth.

"Death is the unknown," the student responded even more confidently.

"If death is the unknown, what is there to fear? Who or what dies?"

"Fear dies, I die, then there is no death," the young student said with certainty.

"Good, you have learned your lesson well, young student. You have conquered your 'self,' fear and death — which are one and the same. Do you understand?" the deep voice queried.

"Yes, sir. I understand what you have taught me. I see that this is the greatest challenge in my Martial Arts training," the student returned, recognizing the figure as his teacher.

"Now, do your form until your mind is empty of all thoughts of fear and death, all thoughts concerning yourself. Stay focused on each movement — as if this is the first time you have performed it. Do not practice out of habit, for then your mind will wander and fear will enter. Does this make sense to you?"

"Yes, sir!" the student replied strongly. And as his teacher watched, sitting quietly on the grass, the student practiced his form with great care. The physical movements were sharp and forceful. His mind was focused intently on each deliberate movement. His teacher watched from among the tombstones in the graveyard on that partially moonlit night. The feeling of fear subsided, and in its place arose calmness. The night was quiet and still. Two figures in a graveyard: one moving in a focused dance, the other watching intently, both in a timeless moment.

We are what we think;
All that we are arises
With our thoughts —
With our thoughts
We make the world.

— Buddha

Never-Ending Maze

Running away from it — it was coming closer and soon he would be devoured — up and away he flew — off the cliff he soared — light as a feather — turning this way and that — in full control — seeing the village below — doing full circles in the air — upside down — it was suddenly following him — on the ground — over bushes — walls — in houses — in basements — trap door — down into a secret room — still following — second trap door — second secret room — still following — along the tunnel — running — running — running — not going anywhere — on the beach — looking at the ocean — watching huge waves — gigantic waves about to crash — running away from waves — not going anywhere — sinking deeper — into the sand — deeper and deeper — waves coming — crashing — turning to face the wave — dive right into it — come up on the other side — again waves — dive again — and again —

"Watch how it takes you," the teacher advised.

Jewelry — rings and necklaces — money — endless money — flowers — food — eating all she wanted — clothes — a store full of clothes — she didn't have any money — there was no one else there — trying on all the clothes — she could have all that she wanted —

"Watch how one thought produces another like it; just watch but don't get involved," the teacher directed. "Be aware of your body as you sit. Are you holding your breath? Breathe. Slowly breathe. Listen to the sounds around you. Feel your body as you sit on the floor. Be aware of the odors in the room. Let all this simply be there. Let the thoughts just happen. They are just one of many sensations you are experiencing. Don't judge them as bad or good. Don't run away from your thoughts, but don't get wrapped up in the pleasure of them either. Just watch. No attachment. And you will begin to see what you are made up of, how the thoughts you have create the world in which you live. You are now looking at the root of all fear and pleasure, the root of conflict. Become attached or run away, and you will be pursued by the Fire Dragon! Get lost in your thoughts and you will be forever caught in an endless maze, lost to the real world, lost in a world of your own making."

The students were sitting quietly facing the wall, heads slightly bowed, hands on their laps, eyes looking down at the floor in front of them. They were breathing slowly.

"And who are you?" asked a voice behind them. The words resounded in their brains among all the bits and pieces of thoughts and images each was experiencing, as they sat observing their minds.

"Who am I? Who am I?" the words echoed back to them. They had been sitting for what seemed like forever. Their legs ached, their backs felt weary and their brains sleepy.

"What are all those thoughts that are running through your heads? Do the thoughts and feelings you are experiencing right now make sense? Or are they merely an endless collection of fears and hopes?" The teacher's voice was strong and focused. The words cut through each one's self-centered thinking, awakening something clear, something untouched by the confusion in their brains.

"Just sitting" was the foundation of the students' Martial Arts practice. They sat each morning. Before they practiced their self-defense forms, they would also sit quietly. And at certain times they would sit for longer periods. It was these longer periods that would bring up the deeper confusion, the many thoughts and feelings that were just fragments and seemed to make no sense.

"Don't try to make sense of what is happening," the teacher instructed. "Just allow it to happen as it does; accept the confusion that arises. Observe what is actually occurring but don't try to change it, to make it orderly, less confusing. Watch these thoughts and feelings as if you are watching a play, one that you don't understand."

The students sat and observed their minds endlessly churning out thoughts. And attached to these thoughts were feelings. The teacher addressed the students at the end of their sitting, saying, "Is this confusion, this maze of thinking, personal? That is, is it yours alone? Or do you realize that it is happening in each one of you, in everyone all the time? Are you aware of certain thoughts that cause greater fear or desire? These stronger thoughts and feelings are the Fire Dragons. They catch you and consume you with ferociousness. They'll burn you up if you get too caught up in them. Beware, there are Fire Dragons at each turn in the maze. They are waiting for the unsuspecting. So don't fall asleep! Wake up! Watch out!"

The teacher paused, then continued, "There is a danger that you will come to believe that the maze is real, that the Fire Dragons are to be fought and killed. These thoughts and feelings create the world, and, in turn, the world affects your thoughts and feelings. The war in our heads, the confusion inside us, creates the war and confusion outside us in the world. See this and you've understood the foundation of all Martial Arts practice, a practice that helps us understand and end our conflict peacefully.

"You students are young and perhaps don't understand all that I am saying. But it is actually very simple. Don't complicate it. Your brains have been filled up with bits and pieces of thoughts. These thoughts come from the past, from what your parents, teachers, friends and books have told you about life. These thoughts have feelings attached to them. If I say 'ice cream,' there is a thought and also a feeling attached to those words. The thought tastes good, so to speak. If I say 'death,' there is a thought associated with that word, and a feeling follows. Perhaps fear. But can you see that this is only a game being played in your brain? This game that your mind plays is called 'association,' which means that your brain connects a thought with a feeling or connects one thought to another thought. If I say "up," you might think *down*; or "river" — *swim*; "fire" — *warmth*; and so on.

"Students, you need to understand how your minds work, to see how thoughts and feelings create your behavior. If you watch what goes on in your brains when you are sitting, you will begin to see the root of conflict. You will begin to see that the thoughts and feelings you have create the world in which you live. If your brain is fearful, then that is exactly what you will create in the world. Oh, students, see the importance of this simple observation! You are the world; the world is you! Violence and wars are created by us, by the way we think and feel. Understand the root of this. Just observe how this occurs, and in understanding this, end it there, before it goes beyond yourself and creates more confusion and violence in the world. It all starts with you! Begin to observe yourself. You can do this at any time. When you are eating, when you are about to go to sleep, or when you are waking up. Just watch and learn. Don't memorize, just keep watching and see what you uncover. Then you can become your own master. You will begin to understand the importance of Martial Arts training and why it is so much more than learning self-defense."

For the next few minutes, the students sat still and watched their thinking and how it functioned in a way common to them all, creating a maze in which they could become lost. They looked into the eyes of many Fire Dragons — and felt the fear or pleasure connected to the thoughts that their brains conjured up. They began to understand their teacher's words, teachings that would lead them to an understanding of "Empty Self," the basis of all Martial Arts.

Inaction is the highest
form of action.

— J. Krishnamurti

Winning by Winning

He moved around her slowly, with the intensity of a lion stalking its prey. His bright eyes were focused, noticing every shift of movement, waiting for an opening so he could attack. Her muscles were tense; she felt heavy and afraid. At the moment of her self-reflection, he leapt forward with a terrifying yell and kicked right at her stomach, and then punched at her face. She fell backwards, not from getting hit, but from the ferociousness of his attack. She came forward once more only to be stalked again by her predator. She felt helpless! He was so strong and overpowering. He was the dominant one, the stronger, the fittest; she felt weak and inferior. What could she do? How could she summon the courage and strength to fight back against such a powerful opponent?

His high powerful side-thrust kick just glanced her arm as she missed her block. Although they were not allowed to make full contact, she was still afraid of getting hurt. Her instructor kept putting her up against this opponent, and each time she would lose, never scoring a single point. As a brown belt she had fought hard to maintain her rank, but he was a first degree black belt! Just seeing the black cloth around his waist made her feel weak and defeated — even before they began their encounter.

"Your mind is too full of fear and thoughts about what might happen," said her teacher after this bout. "Be quiet for the next few days and meditate on nothing but nature around you. Take time off from regular practice and walk into the woods."

Feeling that her teacher wanted to save her from further humiliation, she walked away from the rest of the group and strolled down to the lake near camp. It was late afternoon and the trees were filled with autumn splendor; gold, orange, red, yellow, green leaves carpeted her path. She walked slowly around the lake's edge and then up into the woods. The sun shone on the leaves, accentuating their brilliance. The honking of geese overhead, flying south for the winter, drew her attention upward to the blue sky and the fat white cotton clouds floating above.

The next day she walked again, deeper into the woods, the memory of her defeats still a thorn in her side. Her fears mounted as she reflected on the inevitability of facing her fellow student again. There was no one to talk to; there was only herself. She went over and over her thoughts and fears until she was just too tired to think about them any more. The day was beautiful! She crossed over a small brook, the water moving on to some unseen destination. She could smell the forest, the wet leaves, the pine trees, the fog, and the crisp freshness of nature. Stopping for a moment, she inspected, with affection, a tiny inchworm sunbathing on a yellow birch leaf. The forest was still except for an occasional bird calling and the murmur of wind in the trees. Leaves, like golden snow, were falling softly on the earth and drifting against roots of trees, roots which looked like veins on the forest floor. She noticed a mushroom growing from the side of a moss-covered tree and felt peaceful, calm. All that had happened before drifted away like a leaf in the brook, and what remained was stillness.

Suddenly a feeling arose in her. “It is so simple!” she said out loud, in surprise and joy. “It is so simple!” she repeated as if she needed to pinch herself. “Here is perfect disorder! Nature is what it is. Neither better or worse. What I am looking for is here and has always been here, for it is this very moment itself! I understand everything yet nothing at all!” She quickly turned as a bird sprang from a tree branch into full flight. How effortlessly the bird moved, with such energy! She spent the rest of the day in the woods practicing her forms. Her movements were now effortless and spontaneous. The structured and fixed patterns she had learned through many months of hard practice fell away as a living form rose naturally from within her. As easily as a bird rises in flight, the effortless movements of her form moved her. She became the form; there was only the form; the person and the movement blended into one harmonious whole. Upon returning to the camp in late afternoon, she quietly approached her teacher. “I am ready now!” The teacher looked at her carefully and noted a calmness emanating from her.

The next day this student was put up against her old opponent. She effortlessly moved away from each of his attempts at attack. He tried again and again, but could not score. At the end of the bout, each was scoreless. And yet she had won.

The less effort,
the faster and more powerful
you will be.

— Bruce Lee

Now You See It — Now You Don't!

The chief instructor, whose greatness was legend, entered the fighting area where he was to demonstrate his skills. His attackers were already there, waiting for him. The students were eager; this was a rare opportunity to learn from their master.

The spectators became very still, awaiting his fabled and mysterious Martial Arts techniques. But a strange thing happened. The chief instructor fumbled with tying his black belt which had come undone, seemingly confused as to what was the correct way.

"What is this?" the spectators murmured. *What is he fumbling for? He is weak and afraid,* some thought. "He looks so old and feeble," said another out loud. This giant of a teacher with magical powers seemed all too common now. At the moment that the students perceived his "ordinariness," the chief instructor let out a piercing yell and the attackers went flying in every direction! This chief instructor did indeed possess the skills of a great master. The audience tried to keep up with his movements, but before they could grasp what had happened, the young assistant instructors (the "attackers") were again sprawled out on the ground at the feet of their chief instructor. With great dignity, the master walked steadily from the stage, past his shocked yet unhurt assailants. The demonstration was over.

I have realized that the past and
the future are real illusions,
that they exist only in the present,
which is what there is
and all there is.

— Alan Watts

Not Room for a Single Strand of Hair

The students had just finished a hard workout in self-defense and their uniforms were sopping wet with perspiration. They felt satisfied with their day's accomplishments. The sun was rising high in the sky. Three crows cawed and flew overhead towards the tall dark green pines in the distance. An orange and black caterpillar was crawling ever so slowly along the branch of a nearby tree.

"Your timing was incorrect today," said the teacher, breaking the silence. It was customary for the students and their teachers to discuss their daily self-defense practice.

The teacher suddenly clapped his hands. "Is there any gap between the action of my hands clapping and the sound produced?" the teacher asked. "When you learn to defend yourself from another, are you aware of the gap between the opponent's attack and your response? If there is a gap, your reaction to their action is disconnected. There is no unity. There is a space between the attack and defense. If there is any hesitation, there will be defeat. When there is no gap, no hesitation, the attacker and defender move as one and there is no defeat.

"Now, when your opponent is about to attack you, look for the signals. Look for the attack before it happens and respond appropriately. When you respond to an attack before it happens, not even a strand of hair can enter between you and your opponent."

The students stood up once again and practiced responding to an "attack" without hesitation. The teacher stood in front of the class and raised his hands over his head. When he made a fist, the students were to have already responded. At first there was a gap between the fist and the defense, the response. But as they practiced more and more, they could respond *before* their teacher clenched his fist.

"Now, students, you will not be defeated. Victory is yours. Now when I go to make a fist, run away!"

Without this deeper understanding —
enquiry into the mind —
the Martial Arts merely consist
of a number of gymnastic skills.

— Jean Webster-Doyle

Just Do It!

A Martial Arts master from another school was invited to speak at the camp. Also invited were students from various schools in the area.

As the guest speaker entered, he was greeted with great applause. One student from a nearby school found it hard to contain his jealousy. “I wonder if you are as great a master as people say,” he called out. “You may be able to fool less knowledgeable students and make them do whatever you want, but I have no respect for you. Can you make *me* do what you say?”

“Come here and I will show you,” the visiting master replied. “Come over to the left.” The student went to the left. “On second thought, come to the right.” The student went to the right. “Good,” said the master, “you have obeyed me well. Now sit down and keep quiet.”

Among the greatest things
to be found,
the Being of Nothingness
is by far the greatest.

— Leonardo Da Vinci

Bell Ringing in the Empty Sky

It was evening and the students had gathered around the fire to hear their teachers speak. The stars on this crisp autumn night were brilliant. The fresh air made their spirits rise as they huddled together in anticipation. There was always a soft feeling of affection at these gatherings. A dog was barking in the distance. The wind chimes played softly in the evening breeze, sending melodic tones across the distance. They felt the great mystery of the night. There was just the night, nothing else.

"Students, when we bow, what does this mean? We bow at the door to the school practice area, and we bow before and after practicing our self-defense techniques, and we bow to each other throughout the day as we pass in the yard or in the corridor. Why do we do this? Is it just custom, like a handshake, or is there some deeper significance?"

The woods at night were so dark, but not frightening. The students were now used to the presence of the forest, standing by like a quiet friend. The school cat brushed up against the students' knees, purring as she did so. Each hand in turn reached out and petted her gently.

"What is respect, dear students? Can you tell me?" the teacher asked.

"It is caring for another, teacher. It is thinking about others rather than oneself all the time," responded one student.

"It is having good manners, acting in a way that makes another feel happy," said the next student.

"Respect is to honor someone, to be considerate, and thoughtful, and polite," said a third.

"Respect means to admire someone for their special gifts that they can offer others," said another.

"Then bowing is a formal way to show this respect, this honor, politeness, thoughtfulness. Can you bow naturally without having to be reminded, without any punishment or reward? Can you see the beauty of bowing? How does it feel when another bows to you, not out of habit, but genuinely? Do you feel honored, respected? This, students, is so important in Martial Arts and in daily life. And we so easily forget it. We get so caught up in showing everyone how important we are that we miss the point. But when we bow, we put ourselves aside to greet another. In this we are living the true essence of the Martial Arts: kindness, respect. Does this make sense to you? Watch and find out what the truth of this is."

The cat settled in a student's lap and fell fast asleep. The students sat in silence, reflecting on their teacher's words.

"You thought that the Martial Arts were about defending yourself," the teacher resumed. "Now you know that the Martial Arts are about showing respect."

The wind chimes rang again, sending soft metallic sounds across the water. The moon shone on the still lake. A lone duck landed upon the water, disturbing nothing.

If practiced rightly, the bow becomes the single most important movement in the Martial Arts.

— Terrence Webster-Doyle

Fighting for Peace

One student ran out of the class crying. The others were shocked. Some were on the verge of tears.

"We live in a dream, dear students. Like make-believe warriors, we play soldiers but we don't really know the meaning of what we do," the chief instructor sadly told his students.

"Do you know what it really feels like to get hit in the face, full strength? Can you imagine blinding someone by poking them in the eyes? Or breaking a person's arm or leg, or actually killing them with your self-defense technique? Can you imagine how devastating it would be if you ever had to use your techniques full force?"

The students felt rather sick to their stomachs. They hadn't realized how dangerous and destructive what they had been taught could be. To them, this had all been a fun game. Now it was being made real to them.

"But, sir, I don't want to hurt anyone. I am confused. Why are we practicing these self-defense skills if they can really harm or kill another? What is the sense, the meaning, of all this?" asked a student.

"I certainly don't want to create more violence in the world," the chief instructor confided. "I gave up teaching the Martial Arts once because I felt confused and saddened by the violence I saw in their practice. But I also saw that people need to defend themselves — especially women, unfortunately — against the violence of men. This is a terrible thing to realize."

"What did you do then, teacher?" asked a student.

"I had to find a way to teach people how to defend

themselves if necessary, but also — and more importantly — how to get out of a violent situation without fighting."

"How did you personally learn to get out of dangerous situations without fighting?" asked a new student.

"By gaining the confidence not to fight… because I wasn't afraid any more. Because I had learned how to defend myself, I could think clearly and didn't react automatically, violently."

"Tell us more, please," requested a timid student.

"I would use my mind to get out of the conflict instead of using my fists or feet," the teacher responded.

"In what way would you use your mind?"

"I learned how to use nonviolent alternatives. Have any of you been bullied or threatened with physical violence? What could you do to get out of such a situation without fighting?"

"I could reason with the bully, talk to him or her to find out what the problem is," one student offered.

"What else?" asked the teacher.

"I could run away, but without fear... remove myself from the threat."

"I could try to make friends."

"How about using humor?"

"Or telling the bully that your brother is a Martial Arts expert and that he is to meet you here soon."

"Dear students, we have gone over this before, many times. Most of you have practiced these alternatives. You have role-played both the bully and the victim. We have helped you to act out these peaceful alternatives to reacting violently. But you need to go over them again and again in order to make them second nature. We sometimes spend too much time in self-defense and not nearly enough time on practicing

nonviolent skills. They both go together; self-defense for physical confidence, nonviolent alternatives for mental confidence. Using these together, you can end conflict without hurting yourself or another. Our aim is to resolve conflict."

Let us open our leaves like a flower,
and be passive and receptive.

— Anonymous

Expect the Unexpected

The students were in a circle in ready combat stances. One student was in the middle, standing alert, straight up, hands resting easily at his side. His eyes were soft, not intense. He seemed completely relaxed. He was aware of clouds passing slowly overhead and the pleasant aroma of a fire in the crisp autumn air. A woodpecker, clutching the side of an old tree, was knocking holes into the wood, looking for insects. A large black crow suddenly flew by, cawing.

"One!" called the teacher.

"Kiai!" yelled one of the students in the circle, as she attacked the lone figure in the center.

"Five!" called the teacher again.

"Kiai!" Another student charged forward towards the encircled student.

Each student had been assigned a number. Again and again, the student in the center was attacked as the chief instructor called out a number randomly. Each person, in turn, charged forward to confront the lone student in the center. The student met each attack with the grace and agility of a cat, moving quickly in the direction of each charge.

On and on it went, each person in the circle becoming the victim in the middle. The numbers were called faster or slower, depending on the rank of the student in the center.

At the end of the session, the students sat on the ground and quietly meditated on what had just happened. In each student's mind's eye, each attack and defense was replayed. Running the scenes over and over, each was reviewed as if it were an act in a play.

"Now, students, this is for real!" Each knew what the teacher meant. They had been waiting for this time; they had practiced the circle attack many times over the last few weeks and felt prepared for their test.

"I am going to add something that you did not expect. This will sharpen your skills. Did you think I would make it easy for you, students?!"

The students looked at each other in astonishment. They should have guessed that it would not be as they thought. They had been told over and over, "Expect the unexpected! The moment you think you know what is going to happen, something will change, perhaps only slightly, and catch you off guard. Beware of Fire Dragons. They wait for you to fall asleep, just for a second, and poof! You are burned up." The students listened intently as their teacher outlined a new twist.

"Dear students, you need to be prepared for any attack, whether physical or emotional. If you are alert, you will not be harmed. Physically, you will be able to defend yourself against harm. Mentally, you will be so alert that you will be emotionally protected. No damaging images will be able to get through. You will be wide awake, both mentally and physically. Now, to add something new, to test your balance, the attacker group will not only attack you physically, as we practiced today, but also mentally. They have a choice of attacks. They can choose to attack or befriend you. And you will need to be able to tell the difference. Your attacker can also change, as he or she approaches you, from a seeming attack to greeting you as a friend. Or the opposite: greeting you as a friend and then attacking you. They may also try to hurt you emotionally. This is another kind of attack that is even more vicious. This will happen when you least expect it. It is an attack of the emotions and is very hurtful and dangerous. I will not tell you how they will do this, so you must be extremely aware at all times. Do you understand?" The students sat in silence. Class was over for the day.

It was early evening when the assaults began. Attackers would suddenly charge a student, using combative skills. Again and again, this happened... but nothing else.

That night the students slept little, keeping awake for attacks that they knew would come. And they did, in the dark of the cabins. No light was allowed, so all attacks and defenses were made in complete darkness. The students were excited, awake and alert.

This test was great fun for all, but especially for the new students who had never done this before. However, this game had a serious aspect too. It helped them prepare for real attacks and made them more alert in general. This heightened sense of awareness would help the students to comprehend the deeper issues of conflict.

The next day the attackers tried to confuse the students. What seemed like an attack would become a friendly gesture. An attacker might run up to a student as though in anger and ready to attack. Just as the student began to react in defense, the attacker would break into a smile and give the student a hug. This new approach did confuse the students; they weren't sure how to respond. Sometimes attackers would approach smiling, then suddenly try to punch or kick. The students had trouble responding appropriately. They would mistakenly block a handshake or counterpunch a hug. Sometimes, after extending a hand in friendship, they would find themselves flat on their backs on the ground.

This attack/greeting test went on all that day. At night there was a welcome resting time out. But they all knew that in the morning they would confront thc unknown, the "emotional" attack. This would be even harder to defend against.

The dawn awoke them with a brilliant sun rising over golden tree tops. Birds moved about swiftly, shaking the frosty cold from their tiny bodies. Squirrels ran this way and that, searching for nuts to store for the long winter approaching. They seemed to be playing a game with the dog, running close to her, then up a nearby tree. Each, in turn, would tempt the dog, and then quickly and narrowly escape. The dog was running in circles, trying to be the victor. This was a serious game of life and death, but one that seemed great fun, too.

The students had awakened to the sound of the school bell, as they did each morning. They also retired to their beds upon hearing that wonderful sound. "The bell that rang in the empty sky," they would call it. This bell sounded a tone so beautiful and full that one forgot momentarily where or who one was.

The "attackers" were at breakfast in the dining hall in a group, pointing and laughing at the students on the other side. *What could they be planning? Why are they laughing and pointing?* the students thought nervously. After breakfast, when the students were taking dirty dishes to the kitchen, one of the attackers called out to the group, "Hey, you bunch of cowards! You don't even know how to defend yourselves! You are pitiful. You're wimps!" The students looked at each other in surprise!

As one of the students was quietly leaving the dining hall, an attacker bumped into her, saying, “Girls don’t have a place here studying Martial Arts. Girls are too weak. The Martial Arts were meant for men only.” He shoved past her, leaving her stunned and angry.

Later, one of the students was in the organic garden weeding when an attacker kicked dirt on his uniform, saying in a bullying tone, “Hey, Fatso, can’t you stand up to do that, or are you too heavy? What’s the matter, Fat Boy, can’t take it? Come on, Fatty, why don’t you eat some more, like a pig. Oink, oink!” The student was on the edge of tears as the attacker left the garden, laughing. The student who was indeed overweight, thought sadly, *He’s right. I’m nothing but a big fat pig!*

All day long the attackers insulted and ridiculed the students, calling them hurtful names, making fun of their looks, their family backgrounds, their weaknesses. That night the students asked for a special meeting with their teachers. All the students gathered, including the attackers, who sat together away from the rest of the students.

“We are really upset about how we’re being treated by the attackers,” complained one of the older students. The attackers jeered and booed, then accused the students of being weak and cowardly. The chief instructors and the staff of assistant teachers listened but said nothing.

“They have insulted us. They have called us rude names. They even criticized my family,” said another student in a voice full of emotion. “How can they do this? What happened to manners and affection? We were taught to be kind and respect one another. But this is rude, terrible behavior.”

The attackers kept up the insults. "You students are worthless at the Martial Arts. You are weak and don't belong here with the strong ones," said one of the leaders of the attackers in a boasting way. This comment caused a lot of commotion. The students were losing their composure and beginning to argue back.

"Do I see Fire Dragons?" the chief instructor called out suddenly and loudly. Everyone stopped and there was silence. He repeated his question, "Are there any Fire Dragons in this room?"

"Watch out or you will be burned up!" the other chief instructor called out.

The students looked at each other, then at their teachers, then over at the group of attackers. Everyone was serious and quiet.

"Do you see how you can be so easily attacked and defeated? You have learned how to defend against a physical attack, but when someone attacks you emotionally, calls you names, then you are defenseless," the instructor continued. "Why do you react so to these insults? What causes you to feel hurt and to hurt back? We have talked with you before about this. Do you see the importance of this test? And can you see the problems that such attacks produce? What happens when a group of people is ridiculed? What happens when one group considers themselves superior — or inferior? Can this conflict lead to the most extreme form of conflict: war?"

The students were very quiet for they realized the truth in this lesson.

"What does all this have to do with studying the Martial Arts? Can you see how the seeds of conflict are so easily sown?

If you have an image of yourself, if you have judged yourself, do you see how you leave yourself open to attack? If, for example, you are overweight and someone calls you 'Fatty,' what is an intelligent response? To judge yourself? Do you identify with that name and reinforce the negative image of yourself as a 'fat pig'... in other words, a 'bad' person? Or do you look at the truth or falseness of the statement? You may observe, 'Yes, I am overweight; this is a fact.' Or you will see, 'He is not correct. I am not fat.' Either way, there is no need to defend, to attack your attacker. Do you see how such a situation can become a global problem between nations and groups of people? Let's be silent for a while and reflect on what has happened here between us."

"Today you have learned a very real lesson about the root of conflict. As a Martial Artist, it is your responsibility to understand conflict and how to resolve it peacefully. Physical conflict is an outcome of mental or emotional turmoil, or what is often referred to as 'psychological' conflict. Psychological conflict is at the root of all physical violence. Understand the root and the rest will follow; physical violence will end by understanding that which lies beneath it!"

For the next few days, the psychological attacks continued until the students could hear them without reacting. At first, outward expressions of hurt were still frequent. After a time, the inward hurt was only a shadow, an occasional Fire Dragon raising its ugly head but quickly gone beyond. The students observed their own feelings of hurt as they arose and then faded. They saw that feelings were connected to thoughts, and that thoughts were connected to images which had no real meaning. There was no need to accentuate the hurt, no need to attack. The students eventually learned how to defend themselves against the most difficult psychological attacks by not defending. They also became adept at expecting the unexpected.

When you seek it,
you cannot find it.

— Old Saying

Opening the Door to Wisdom

The chief instructor was sitting inside his room when he heard a knock on the door.

"Who is there?" the teacher called out.

"It is student Miguel," replied the student.

"Go away!" the teacher responded. The student went away but came back the next day.

The student went up to the door and knocked again.

"Who is it?" called out the teacher.

"It is I, student Miguel," the student replied again.

"Go away!" the teacher responded again.

This kept up for two more days. On the night preceding the fourth day, the student sat quietly for a long while in silent meditation. Then, at dawn, the student walked over to his teacher's door and knocked again.

"Who is there?" the teacher called out.

"Nobody," the student replied.

The door opened and there stood his teacher smiling. "Oh, dear student, please come in."

If you are not happy here and now,
you never will be.

— Taisen Deshimara

There is No First Attack

"You have only one chance to attack. You will have two minutes in which to deliver an attack and to score a full point. Defenders, you must try to stop the attack before it happens. Attackers, you must give everything to your attack. You each have only one encounter, and you each have only one chance. As in life, there are no rehearsals. Everything is real, now. There is no going back, no correcting mistakes. The past is gone in a flash and the future never gets here. So what are you to do — now?"

"Begin!" commanded the assistant instructor at the center of the ring. The two students, after bowing and assuming their ready stances, moved quickly but cautiously into fighting stances. Slowly and carefully they moved around each other, waiting for the right moment — that space of inattention where one could enter in and score. Or that moment of perception of an intent, just as it was beginning to happen.

For what seemed like forever, the two moved together. One stayed in the center, following the one who encircled him. Then, with great suddenness and blinding speed, there was a rapid motion between the two and it was over.

"Stop!" called the assistant instructor. "You successfully perceived the attack," she said to one of the students. "You ended it before it started. This is the meaning of 'One Encounter, One Chance.' This is the skill necessary to end all conflict: to be alert enough to perceive and end conflict before it happens."

The cat lying on the deck suddenly sprang forward from its resting place to grab a leaf as it flew by. Investigating its prey, it played with it for a minute, then let it go, as easily as it had come. The cat walked off slowly, as if nothing had happened, and settled comfortably again in a sunny corner of the yard outside the practice hall.

A rose is a rose is a rose.

— Gertrude Stein

Art of Silence

It had been a very cold night. The trees were losing their leaves faster now. The wind blew them in swirls in a multi-colored dance. The season's first brush of snow graced the tops of the majestic hills. More geese, in a wavering V-formation, were flying south in a cloudless sky of brilliant blue, honking their way, following unseen guidance.

"What you tell us, teachers, is sometimes hard for us to understand. You speak of 'Empty Self' and fear and death and peace in the world. And of what we can do to end war.... But many times we are not sure about what you are saying. At times, it makes sense and at other times we are confused."

"Students, you are young and we don't expect you to understand everything we tell you. However, we do know that you can eventually understand everything we say. But don't expect it to be easy. Was it easy to learn your self-defense forms? It took time and you had to work at it. The same is true with understanding conflict, war and peace. You have to work at it! But if you do, if you really want to understand, if you are serious, then you can find out. And as you do, you will begin to realize the tremendous implications of your study here. But remember, don't believe in what we tell you. Find out for yourself by questioning, by using your mind. Educate your mind as well as your body; there needs to be a balance between the two. That muscle between your ears must to be exercised daily! Accepting what we tell you without question will lull your brain to sleep. Then you will live in a world of dreams and, I'm afraid, nightmares. So wake up, students, and see the truth for yourselves. No one can do it for you."

"We will work hard at finding out for ourselves," said a young student earnestly. The others nodded in agreement.

The dog was barking loudly outside and chasing squirrels. A spider was delicately spinning an intricate web in the corner of the window, a beautifully patterned survival net.

"Today we will play a Martial Arts game, one that requires the highest skill. This skill cannot be practiced like self-defense forms. This skill cannot be thought up, copied, or learned from another. It can only happen when all effort ceases, all trying stops. And yet you have to try and do it! I hope I am not confusing you!" the teacher said with a broad smile, his wise eyes sparkling.

"Now, I want you to form a circle. I need a volunteer to be the first subject. Please stand in the center of the circle and put this blindfold on. Now slowly turn around and around until I tell you to stop. Stop!" The student stood quietly, listening for the next instructions from his teacher.

"Now students, when I point to you, I want you to move very, very quietly towards the student in the middle, not giving any indication that you are moving. The student in the middle will try to locate where this movement towards him is by pointing in that direction. If the student in the middle is correct, then the person coming forward will go back and we will start over with another person. I will not tell the student in the middle if she or he is correct; the student in the middle must 'know.' You must be able to feel, sense, be aware of the student coming at you, without using the senses of hearing, seeing or touching."

"If the student in the middle is not correct, the student moving forward will keep coming until the student advancing can touch the student in the center. Now let's try it. Afterwards, we will discuss what this exercise means in the Martial Arts."

The student in the center stood very quietly, listening intently for any signal. Barely breathing, he paid attention to every slight movement or noise. Sounds of birds outside, floors creaking, the wind occasionally blowing up against the window, the fire crackling — each tiny sound became amplified. His heartbeat sounded loudly; even another's swallowing was noticeable. And every little itch or pain became almost unbearable as the game progressed.

Each student had a turn to be in the middle. Sometimes a person was caught moving forward, sometimes not. The real intent of the game became evident. Through heightened silent alertness or sensitivity, the students were becoming aware of their capacity to understand at another level — a level beyond thinking or reasoning. This level was "observation"... and it brought to light the ability to be aware, to understand oneself and another in the moment, without reasoning it out.

As if by an unusual magnifying glass, their sensitivities were greatly heightened so that they became aware of things they were not usually aware of. And in having to sense someone moving forward towards them, they learned that they had a built-in detector that allowed them to stop someone from coming too close to them.

"What did you notice in this exercise?" the teacher asked. Each student, in turn, spoke of what he or she had not previously been aware of. And each was especially surprised at being able to sense when someone was just about on top of them, without seeing or hearing or touching.

"Student, come walking slowly towards me," the teacher directed one of the students. "There, stop! You are just about to enter my personal safety circle. Each one of us has this circle. If you extend your arm out, you will see where the edge of this circle is... usually an arm's length plus a few inches. You can invite friends into this circle or keep them out. That's up to you. It is your circle, a field of energy surrounding you which helps you sense who or what you want to keep out or let in."

All of the students practiced walking towards each other to find out where their personal circles were.

"Now, why do we do this exercise? What meaning does it have to you, in both your Martial Arts training and in your daily life? You started out today's session by telling us how hard it is to understand everything we are teaching. You realized that you have to work at it, that you have to really want to find out, that you must question and find out for yourselves. It is also true that you must be sensitive, alert, perceptive to all that is around you, without relying on thinking, hearing, seeing or touching. Sensitivity. There is a very practical need for sensitivity, to 'feel' what another is intending. You can 'feel' if something is correct, or true, or not. You can 'feel' what is dangerous and what is friendly. This is built into you; you are born with it. You can nurture this sensitivity as you would a little seedling just planted. You can give it water and sunlight, and then it will simply grow on its own. Sensitivity is like that little seedling; it needs care, but not force. This sensitivity helps you to be aware of, to 'feel,' conflict in yourself or another. Just be aware of conflict when it happens, without doing anything about it. Try it and find out what happens. See what happens to conflict when it is perceived with sensitivity, with 'affection.' Also see what happens when thought enters and judges, as we have been so often taught to do. See the difference between silent awareness and judgment in understanding and going beyond conflict."

Noticing some questions on the students' faces, the teacher added, "Remember, find out for yourself the meaning of all this. It may seem much too hard for you right now. But as you begin to find out, it all becomes so very simple. Ending conflict seems to be impossible. But it isn't impossible — in fact, it is very possible!"

People sleep, and when they die, they wake.

— Muhammad

Chains of Freedom

The river ran swift over rocks polished clean and smooth from years of movement. Willow tree branches bent low, touching the bank. A rabbit scampered out of the undergrowth to stop suddenly and stand completely still, except for its twitching nose. Its ears were perked straight up, listening for any sound. A steel gray day reflected the moody, almost leafless trees. The ground was cold and wet from a storm the night before. The growth of nature slowed; animals scurried about gathering food for the long, scarce season to come. In a clearing on two large rocks sat one of the chief instructors and a lone student.

"Teacher, what is the way to freedom? How can we be free of our fear, our pain, our pleasure and desires? For there is great sorrow in all this," the student enquired sincerely.

The teacher closed her eyes for a moment and seemed to be asleep, or resting. When she opened them a few moments later, she said, "Show me your chains."

The student replied with a surprised look on his face, "Teacher, I don't have any chains!"

"Then why are you seeking freedom?" the teacher replied softly with a kind smile.

The bird of paradise alights
only upon the hand
that does not grasp.

— John Berry

The Secret of the Martial Arts

The student was on his knees polishing the old wooden floor of the practice hall when in walked one of the chief instructors. Every day the floor was swept, washed and polished, until it shone brightly. Years of polishing had worn down the wood so that the natural lines and cracks were revealed, uncovering a magnificent natural pattern.

Each student was assigned a task for the week. Each task was an honor that the students took on with pride. However, at first this was not so. Many new students resisted chores, but after a while they began to appreciate the beauty of cleanliness and order. It made them feel good inside. Polishing the practice hall floor was a special honor and was given to those who showed great promise.

Pausing, the student bowed from a kneeling position towards his teacher. She, in turn, bowed while standing. The student spoke, "Excuse me, teacher. May I discuss something with you?"

"Yes, student, please do," replied the teacher, sitting down across from her student.

"Teacher, I have been searching and searching for the secret to the Martial Arts and therefore to life."

"I know that," the teacher replied.

"Do you know the secret of the Martial Arts and of life?" the student responded excitedly and with great expectation!

"Yes, I know that," the teacher replied again.

"Please, teacher, tell me the secret to the Martial Arts and of life!"

“Oh, I couldn’t do that!” said the teacher with a smile.
“Why not?” the student questioned.
“Because it’s a secret,” the teacher answered.

Everyone is in the best seat.

— John Cage

Sound of the Dragon's Fury

They were walking through the woods at night. Only two lanterns lit their way: one at the head of the line and one at the end. Tonight they were to meet the Fire Dragon within themselves, to hear the sound of the Dragon's Fury. It was a night they would never forget.

The two yellow lanterns pierced the darkness. Shadowed figures in uniforms walked in a long line, winding their way along a leaf-packed path. The tall trees, now barren, were like boney fingers reaching up from the earth towards the sky. The cold evening caused them to shiver and rub themselves to create warmth.

One of the chief instructors led the way, while another instructor watched the end for stragglers. They walked in silence for over an hour, until they came to a small clearing that sloped downward to a group of large boulders. They all moved forward toward the dark, massive rocks. As they got closer, they noticed a large opening in the boulders, a cave entrance. The group stopped. Suddenly there was a flurry of motion as hundreds of dark flying creatures came darting out of the cave's entrance and disappeared into the black night. The students' eyes were wide in anticipation of what was to come.

"Inside, students, the Fire Dragon awaits in all its fury. You will be tested for courage and tonight you will need it!" The students shivered, partially from the cold, and partially due to their teacher's brief comment. They were led inside the cave.

They noticed that the walls were high. An old, wet, musky smell enveloped them upon entering. On the ceiling were dark

spots the size of large hands. The chief instructor raised her lantern while the other teacher clapped his hands. The walls and ceiling came alive suddenly as the hand-sized black spots flew off and around them.

"Bats!" one of the students blurted out. "Yeow," another one exclaimed.

"Quiet, students. They will settle down again when we move on."

Down a dark, slippery passageway, they moved deeper into the cave, away from the friendly night outside. They climbed down through another opening and entered a room large enough for all of them to move freely about without any hindrance.

"You have only one weapon down here, and that is your *kiai*," their teachers instructed. The students remembered the lesson earlier that day on *kiai*, that special Martial Arts "yell" that is used when applying a technique.

"The *kiai* shout or yell does two things," their teacher had said. First, it helps make a self-defense technique stronger by tightening your stomach muscles when you block, punch, throw or kick. But the *kiai* also has another application which is a little harder to understand." The students had listened with great interest, for they had seen the power of the *kiai* in practice.

"The *kiai* can also be used to stop your opponent from hurting you by scaring or shocking him or her. Like being hit with a bucket of freezing cold water — it wakes you up! It brings a person out of the dream world, out of the nightmare they are living. It is an important tool for survival. Tonight you will actually experience what this second application of *kiai* means. You will need it when you confront the Fire Dragon's fury!" The words echoed in the students' heads. They were brought back suddenly to the cave when the lanterns went out.

For what seemed like forever, no one said anything. The students had been instructed not to talk, and the two chief instructors were silent. The dark was so complete that the students could not see their hands in front of their faces. There was absolutely no light whatsoever! And no sound. Everyone was standing stark still. Very slowly, little by little, something was beginning to grow in that stone room deep in that cave below the earth. It began to grow larger and larger. Each student could feel it grow, could sense its ominous presence. No one dared move. The students were hardly aware of the others in that immense dark. Each one seemed completely alone! And something was growing, taking over all the space inside that cave. It grew so large that each one felt suffocated by its overpowering presence. It was the Fire Dragon! Intense and overwhelming fear! Fear so great that they all wanted to scream and run in any and all directions. The Fire Dragon had complete control over them. They could not stop it. Then suddenly, out of that tomb of complete blackness, the students heard the loudest and deepest yell they had ever heard in their lives. It was a grand *kiai*. Like a great tidal wave, it rose up from the depths of the soul. Out it came and echoed so fully in that cave that the fear vanished in a split second. The Fire Dragon ceased to exist in the blast of that *kiai*! And again, another *kiai* bellowed forth with tremendous power and strength. A mighty courageous shout, a tremendous yell that shook the walls and their brains. The feared Fire Dragon was on the run.

"Kiai!"

"Kiai!"

Each *kiai* was followed by another and another, until the cave seemed to lift up out of darkness, and the sky seemed to reach down to them. Before they realized it, they were up on the surface again, with the cave below still echoing with the sound of the fury of the *kiai*.

The full moon rose before them. They all felt great energy pulsing through their bodies, and they could see clearly into the night. There was no fear left. They walked without the light of lanterns back to camp. Each one had a new-found strength that they would never forget nor lose.

To know that you do not know
is the best.
To pretend to know
when you do not know
is disease.

— Lao Tzu

The Perfect Master

The teacher was getting a tea cup off the shelf when he heard a knock on the door.

"Come in," he replied gently.

"Good day, Sir. I have your afternoon tea here." The student put the tray down on the low table. She looked around the room and saw how plain it was, and yet she felt the great beauty of this simple cabin.

"Won't you join me for tea?" he asked the student.

"Thank you, teacher, I appreciate the invitation from such a great and perfect master as you."

The teacher smiled at hearing such grand words from the student.

As they sat, slowly sipping their tea, the student noticed that there were no pictures on the walls, except for one of a vase of flowers.

"Do you not have a picture of your great and perfect master, your own teacher, the one from whom you learned?" asked the student politely.

"Oh, certainly. It is most important that I see the great master who knows all each day," replied the teacher, smiling behind his words. "Look there, behind the curtains, and you will see the perfectly enlightened master."

The student rose, walked over to the curtain, and drew it aside to find herself looking in a mirror.

The Kingdom of God is within you.

— Luke, 17:21

Mind — Breath — Body

The dawn was cold and clear. The dark slowly gave way to light, a natural transition without interruption. It was a time of quietness. The birds hadn't begun to stir yet and the moon still floated in the sky. The earth was solid, hard, and rough underfoot as the students and teachers padded quietly along the short path to the open meadow practice area. The mist of early morning surrounded them. They were still warm from sleep and didn't mind the cold. The brief exercise period each morning woke them up for the day.

Coming to the clearing, the students and assistant instructors spread out to find enough space for each one of them to move freely. The sun was beginning to rise at the edge of the earth. Occasionally, a bird moved, flying from tree to tree. The snow would soon completely disappear.

"Today, we will learn how to think, breathe and move. This is called Mind—Breath—Body and is an important part of your Martial Arts training," said one of the instructors, breaking the silence.

"The breath is like water — strong, powerful — and the body is like rock, earth or mountain. The mind creates a thought which is passed on to the body: a message to move, act. For example, when you block, throw or practice a form, most of the time there is only the thought and the action. The action happens because of will power, because you want it to happen. And therefore you use a lot of muscle power to get what you want. But there is something else that will allow you to act more powerfully, with less effort, and this is the breath. Now try this experiment. Get a partner and stand behind that person. Lift them straight up from their elbows. You will have to bend down some, put your hands up underneath their bent arms at the elbow, and push upward. Now I have given your mind a command, which is a thought. You must carry out your thought. Do it."

Each student took a turn at trying to lift a partner by the elbows. Some could lift all the way because they were physically stronger than the others. Some could only lift part way, and others had a hard time lifting at all.

"Now, listen to me. We are going to add the breath. Trying to lift someone with thought alone is like the wind trying to move mountains. It takes a hurricane to do anything at all. A lot of unnecessary effort is used. But if you add the breath between the idea and the action, you add the strength of water. The breath is very powerful and doesn't require muscle. So, now listen to my directions. Think of lifting your partner. Bend down, put your hands on their elbows, keeping your elbows tight against your body, and use your breath as a lever to lift. Lift with your breath! Use a long, drawn out *kiai*, but deeper, smoother, from below the stomach. Now try it."

Each, in turn, tried to lift their partner again, using a long *kiai*. And to their amazement, they found it much easier this time. Some still couldn't lift all the way, but they could lift farther than before and with more ease.

"You are aware of the power of the *kiai*, the short, strong yell used to create extra strength by contracting the abdominal muscles. This is somewhat the same, but is longer, stretched. There is much to learn about the breath, the *ki* in *kiai*. As you study, you will see how breathing calms, cools, invigorates and strengthens the mind and body. *Ki* gives vitality and inner strength to living. Remember, self-defense is a very small part of your practice. Studying the Martial Arts is a lifetime's work that will help you in everything you do. Your life will be healthier, physically and mentally. Now, let's practice again. Mind —Breath — Body; Mind — Breath — Body."

The mind of a perfect man
is like a mirror.
It grasps nothing. It expects nothing.
It reflects but does not hold.
Therefore, the perfect man can act
without effort.

— Chuang Tzu

Doing Nothing

Two students were walking one afternoon after practice when they came to a small hill above a clearing. There, looking out over the forest lands and valley below, they saw one of their chief instructors not far away.

"I wonder what he is doing there all alone," said one.

"He is probably waiting for someone," said the other.

"No! It seems more like he's looking for something," said the first.

"No! I'm sure he's waiting for someone!" the second student repeated.

"Well, why don't we ask him?" exclaimed the first. The two students walked on to where their teacher was standing.

"Excuse me, teacher, would you mind telling us what you're doing here?" asked one of the students politely.

"I don't mind," responded the teacher looking at his students. "I am standing on this hill."

No object is mysterious.
The mystery is your eye.

— Elizabeth Bowen

Speak No Evil

"You are now at the end of this camp. We wonder what you have learned about yourself and the Maze of the Fire Dragon."

The practice hall was lit with candles dripping wax on wooden holders. Shadows danced on the walls, flickering in a never-ending motion. All the students, assistant instructors, and the two chief instructors were present. They all felt stronger physically and clearer mentally than when they had arrived. It had been a long time of challenge and learning. Each student felt more mature, intelligent. It was as if each had grown up during their stay. An older student had once told them that life is a continuous process of growing up, of being a touch wiser than before — that is, if one is serious and works at it.

"Teachers," one of the senior students began, "you have taught us much. We have lived, shared food, worked, studied, and grown together. What we now realize is that there is no point in life where one can stop and say, 'I know all there is to know. I don't need to go any farther.'" The whole group listened as this older senior student spoke from his heart.

"We have begun to understand what the challenges of life are, how there are many traps along the way, many 'Fire Dragons' that can catch up with us and consume us. We have begun to see how our brains are filled with thoughts and feelings that have been conditioned into us by our families, friends, books, our cultures. We see that although our brains are filled with these thoughts and feelings, we don't have to act on them; we can be free of their influence."

Each student felt that this student was speaking the truth, that what he had observed and learned was true for them all — that the 'Maze of the Fire Dragon' represents something that everyone faces, that this is not just one individual's dilemma. This insight helped them to look at the whole situation without personal attachment, and without the feeling of being isolated from other people.

"We realize, teachers, that we are the world, and the world is us, that we are responsible. We create reality through how and what we think and feel. This is a great insight. We understand more fully how to deal with conflict, not only in our daily lives but also in the world. We understand that we create war and that we can end it. We see now how the Martial Arts can help us understand the great concerns of people everywhere. And we are only beginning to glimpse the great value in what we have been taught. It has been difficult, and we are still struggling to understand much of what you have shown us. We feel confident that we can understand and end conflict. We are now aware that this is possible. And for all of this, we thank you."

The hall was silent. For a few minutes, everyone sat quietly, reflecting on all that had transpired.

"Now, end it! Don't look back! Forget what you think is right or wrong!" one of the chief instructors suddenly thundered. "Expect the unexpected! Keep alert. Watch, observe, and learn as you go, but don't get attached to what you see — neither fear it nor want it. Pain and pleasure are the Double-Edged Sword. You will get hurt by either side. Do you understand? Tell me so and I will know that you do not understand. Do not tell me and you will be caught up endlessly in the Maze of the Fire Dragon. What do you say?" he cried out.

The senior student let out a great and powerful *"kiai!"* — jumping up into combat position. All the students followed as one body. The hall resounded with a great wave of energy. Not even a single strand of hair could enter between them. As the sound subsided, the students sat down, facing the wall, with legs crossed. Each one placed their hands in their lap, looked down at the floor, straightened their back and watched.
Just watched.

And as the river flows
So it goes
On and on
From nothing to nothing.

To be continued —

To the Young Reader

You have just finished the second in the Martial Arts for Peace Series: "Tales of the Empty-Handed Masters." If you are unclear about something in this book, please direct your questions to a trusted teacher, a parent, or a wise friend — or write to me (my address follows). It is good to question. Through questioning, you will find out for yourself what is true and what is not true. Don't believe what is written here! Belief is dangerous. Take it upon yourself to find out. This may be hard work and many people will not want to try. But as Martial Artists, we are used to challenges. We invite learning, no matter how difficult, because learning is life. Without learning, one would go to sleep and live in the maze, lost to the real world, entangled in self-made dreams of pleasure and pain. The real world is of immense beauty! Nothing can compare. How do you know this to be true? How will you find out? It's up to you — but remember, there will be kind teachers along the way who will act as signposts.

To the Adult Reader

Teachers, Educators, Parents,
Counselors, School Administrators

Martial Arts as Education for Peace in the 21st Century

The most important view of this book, and all my books, is that we *can* understand and end conflict, individually and globally. The wars that have plagued human beings for thousands of years *can* end if we are serious about understanding their *cause.*

Too often we have approached trying to resolve conflict intellectually. We turn to authorities — psychologists, philosophers, religious leaders, politicians, sociologists, historians, anthropologists, and on and on — for solutions to the problems of human relationship. We have given up our own power of understanding. We have been conditioned to believe that we average people need authorities to solve our problems of relationship. I question this assumption!

I think that the only person who can solve our problems is each one of us. We create our own problems and the problems in the world. We have to find out for ourselves what is true or not true, what works and what doesn't. In looking to authorities for the solution, we can only follow an *ideal*: an intellectual explanation or a moral commandment. Either one paradoxically creates more conflict because each leads to judgment of actual behavior and the idealization of a desired behavior — which is divisive and only creates more conflict.

The thing that we can do is to examine the problem *as it actually happens*! And that is in the moment itself — not through hindsight nor foresight, but now, as it occurs. The faculty that is needed that will "solve" our problems of relationship is insight, or intelligence — the ability to see, to observe, to be aware of what is occurring as it happens. In order to understand conflict, we must not theorize or moralize about it. We must come into direct contact with it, observing its movement, its nature and its structure in operation.

The Martial Arts can play an important role in the observation of the workings of conflict for — after all — they are the arts of war, of conflict. A Martial Art, if taught rightly, can be a valuable context within which to explore the actual movement of conflict.

ABOUT THE AUTHOR

Dr. Terrence Webster-Doyle, Founder and Chief Instructor of Take Nami Do Karate and the Director of the Shuhari Institute — A Center for the Study of the Martial Arts, has studied and taught Karate for over 30 years, has a doctorate degree in psychology, and is a credentialed secondary and community college instructor. He earned his Black Belt in the Japanese style of Gensei Ryu Karate from Sensei Numano in 1967. He has worked in Juvenile Delinquency Prevention, taught at the university level in education, psychology and philosophy, and developed counseling programs for young people. Dr. Webster-Doyle is currently the Director of the Atrium Society. He and his wife Jean are co-parenting five daughters.

Dr. Terrence Webster-Doyle and Rod Cameron can be contacted through the Atrium Society. (See address and phone number on facing page.)

ABOUT THE ARTIST

Rod Cameron was born in 1948 in Chicago, Illinois, but has lived in Southern California most of his life. He studied painting with the renowned illustrator, Keith Ward, and at the Otis/Parsons School of Design in Los Angeles, California.

Rod has been designing and illustrating for over 20 years; his work has been shown on major network television and has received 17 awards for illustrative excellence.

ABOUT THE PUBLISHER

Atrium Society concerns itself with fundamental issues which prevent understanding and cooperation in human affairs. Starting with the fact that our minds are conditioned by our origin of birth, our education and our experiences, the intent of the Atrium Society is to bring this issue of conditioning to the forefront of our awareness. Observation of the fact of conditioning — becoming directly aware of the movement of thought and action — brings us face-to-face with the actuality of ourselves. Seeing who we actually are, not merely what we think we are, reveals the potential for a transformation of our ways of being and relating.

If you would like more information, please write or call us. We enjoy hearing from people who read our books and we appreciate your comments.

Atrium Society
P.O. Box 816
Middlebury, Vermont 05753
Tel: (802) 388-0922
Fax: (802) 388-1027
For book order information:
(800) 848-6021

ABOUT THE SHUHARI INSTITUTE

The intention of the Shuhari Institute is to bring together the people and resources that give an intelligent perspective to the Martial Arts, and to disseminate thought-provoking and insightful information about its creative aspects through literature, videotapes, classes, workshops and conferences. Dr. Webster-Doyle conducts workshops in New England, and in other areas upon request. For more information, contact the Atrium Society. (See address and phone number above.)

BOOKS by Dr. TERRENCE WEBSTER-DOYLE

— *For Adults* —

Karate: *The Art of Empty Self*
One Encounter, One Chance: *The Essence of the Art of Karate*

THE "SANE AND INTELLIGENT LIVING" SERIES

Growing up Sane: *Understanding the Conditioned Mind*
Brave New Child: *Education for the 21st Century*
The Religious Impulse: *A Quest for Innocence*
Peace—The Enemy of Freedom: *The Myth of Nonviolence*

— *For Young People* —

THE "EDUCATION FOR PEACE" SERIES (AGES 7-15)

Why is Everybody Always Picking on Me?: *A Guide to Handling Bullies*
Fighting the Invisible Enemy: *Understanding the Effects of Conditioning*
Tug of War: *Peace Through Understanding Conflict*
Operation Warhawks: *How Young People Become Warriors*

THE "MARTIAL ARTS FOR PEACE" SERIES (AGES 10-17)

Facing the Double-Edged Sword: *The Art of Karate for Young People*
Why is Everybody Always Picking on Me?: *A Guide to Handling Bullies*
Eye of the Hurricane: *Tales of the Empty-Handed Masters*
Maze of the Dragon: *Tales of the Empty-Handed Masters*
Flight of the Golden Eagle: *Tales of the Empty-Handed Masters*
Breaking the Chains of the Ancient Warrior:
Tests of Wisdom for Young Martial Artists

International Praise for Dr. Terrence Webster-Doyle's Previous Books for Young People — the "Education for Peace" Series:

The award winning "Education for Peace" books have earned widespread acclaim as resources for the understanding and nonviolent resolution of conflict.

- Dr. Webster-Doyle has been awarded the Robert Burns Medal for Literature by Austria's Albert Schweitzer Society, for "outstanding merits in the field of peace-promotion."

- "Dr. Webster-Doyle takes the reader beyond the physical aspects of Karate training to a discovery of self. These books are an asset to Martial Arts instructors, students and parents of all styles, ages and rank levels."
  — Marilyn Fierro, 6th Dan
  Owner and Chief Instructor
  Smithtown Karate Academy, Smithtown, NY

- Winner of Benjamin Franklin Award for Excellence in Independent Publishing

- "These topics are excellent and highly relevant. If each of the major countries of the world were to have ten Drs. Webster-Doyle, world peace is guaranteed to be achieved over a period of just one generation."
  — Dr. Chas. Mercieca, Executive Vice-President
  International Ass'n of Educators for World Peace
  NGO, United Nations (ECOSOC), UNICEF & UNESCO

- Acclaimed at the Soviet Peace Fund Conference in Moscow and published in Russia by Moscow's Library of Foreign Literature and Magistr Publications

- "Every publication from the pen of this author should make a significant contribution to peace within and without. Highly recommended!"
  — *New Age Publishers and Retailers Alliance Trade Journal*

- ***Why is Everybody Always Picking on Me?*** — cited by the *Omega New Age Directory* as one of the "Ten Best Books of 1991" for its "atmosphere of universal benevolence and practical application." Recommended by The National PTA, 1995; Instructor Magazine, 1994; and Scouting Magazine, 1992.

HOW TO USE THESE BOOKS IN A MARTIAL ARTS PROGRAM

Dr. Webster-Doyle's books can add quality and spirit to Martial Arts programs and are available at bulk discounts to Martial Arts schools and organizations. The books have been widely used:

- As part of the introductory membership package for new students
- As required reading for rank advancement
- As awards for performance or improvement
- As books for sale in the school's store
- As available reading in the school library
- As material to read aloud and discuss during class

ORDERING INFORMATION

To learn more about Atrium Society Publications' special discounts for Martial Arts programs, to place orders, or to request a free catalog, please write or call:

Atrium Society Publications / Shuhari Institute
P.O. Box 816
Middlebury, Vermont 05753
Toll Free: 1-800-848-6021

Dr. Webster-Doyle is available for workshops in your area.
Please contact us at the above address.

JOSIAH TRUE AND THE ART MAKER

JOSIAH TRUE AND THE ART MAKER

By
Amy Littlesugar

Illustrated by
Barbara Garrison

Simon & Schuster Books for Young Readers

The artwork for this book are collagraphs. The word "collagraph" is from the words "collage" and "graphic." A collagraph plate is made up of pieces of paper and other materials glued down on cardboard, which is then inked and printed on an etching press. Once dried, watercolor washes are applied for color.

SIMON & SCHUSTER BOOKS FOR YOUNG READERS
An imprint of Simon & Schuster Children's Publishing Division
1230 Avenue of the Americas, New York, New York 10020

Book design by Paul Zakris.
The text for this book is set in 13 1/2-point New Aster.
Manufactured in the United States of America
10 9 8 7 6 5 4 3 2 1

Library of Congress Cataloging-in-Publication Data
Littlesugar, Amy.
Josiah True and the art maker / by Amy Littlesugar ;
illustrated by Barbara Garrison.
p. cm.
Summary: An itinerant woman artist comes to paint the True family's
portrait and makes a special brush for Josiah before she leaves.
[1. Artists—Fiction. 2. Painting—Fiction.] I. Garrison, Barbara, ill.
II. Title.
PZ7.L7362Jo 1995 [E]—dc20 946834 CIP AC
ISBN: 0-671-88354-2

For David

—A. L.

To Gilberto Guerrero Sanchez
and Frederico Lopez-Castro, who
introduced me to "collagraphia"

—B. G.

Early morning in the marketplace found Josiah True and his father selling off a spring flock of fattened goslings, a sow and six piglets, and ten baskets of extra corn that Thomas True had planted in the southwest meadow.

With money to spare, they set out for the silversmith's shop, where they read with interest this sign:

PORTRAIT PAINTING—To Your Liking
Only 5 to 10 Dollars each.
Inquire soon, As I will be off before October
Is under way—Signed, Miss Patience Cage / Art Maker

Only
5 to 10

Josiah had heard about the art maker.

Each spring she would carefully load a wagon with her artist's tools, traveling to wherever she had heard a portrait might be wanted.

She painted a fine likeness of Thora Sweet, who was one hundred and one.

She painted the twin sons of Augustus Jones, a sea captain and nephew of Mrs. Sweet.

She painted the only baby of the Reverend and Mrs. Ezekiah Gray, distant cousins of Captain Jones.

She had even painted a proud Mohegan man, who lived in the forest not far from the Reverend Gray's meetinghouse.

Now about this time, the swineherd's wife stopped at the silversmith's as well. She wore a yoke across her shoulders, balanced by two tipping buckets.

"Where is Patience Cage?" she asked. "I have brought the art maker fresh linseed oil to make more paint, and soft hog bristle to mend her broken brushes."

"Here I am," said the art maker from a great height.

Josiah was surprised to see how tall the art maker was, and remembered a village story he had heard about her.

In the story, bandits had come upon Patience Cage on one of her journeys. Believing her wagon to be filled with gold instead of paint, they demanded that she step down from her wagon. But the art maker fixed upon them such clear gray eyes that one was moved to say, "Why, she can see into the very soul of a man!" Frightened, they left Patience to her traveling.

Josiah could hardly wait for the art maker to paint his family's portrait. A handshake between his father and Patience Cage sealed the contract.

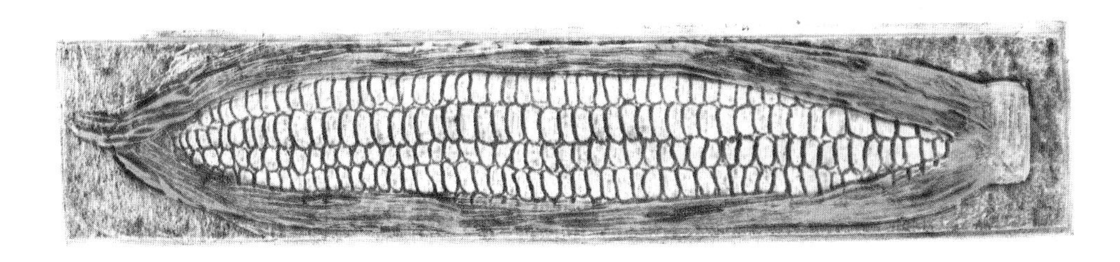

The next morning, the art maker's wagon came rolling up the road to the True farm.

Patience Cage was going to paint the family portrait in a small room with a white settee between two windows.

Josiah's mother, Eliza Bascom True, would be seated on the settee. She wanted to be painted in a red gown, which she did not own. Thomas True would stand behind his wife. He wanted to wear a new waistcoat, which he did not own. Josiah would be seated, with his legs crossed, on the floor at his mother's feet. He wished that he owned a brave watchdog with a golden collar.

The art maker promised them that they would see all of these things in the portait she painted.

Josiah helped her unload the wagon.

In it there was a stack of small wooden panels for one-person portraits, as well as large frames stretched drumhead tight with linen cloth. These were for family portraits.

There was a three-legged easel made of birch. Tied to one of the legs was a painting stick to keep the art maker's brush strokes steady and straight.

The last thing in the wagon was a heavy box stenciled in gold. This the art maker carried into the house herself.

Patience Cage began the portrait by setting up her easel and canvased frame. On a nearby table, she opened the box and shared its treasures with Josiah. Not a space had been spared! There were paintbrushes the art maker had made over the winter, bottles of powdered color, and many small leather pouches of paint made by mixing the linseed oil and colors together.

There was a palette for laying out her paints, a knife for scraping it clean, cloth and turpentine and sticks of charcoal.

Then she began posing the True family.

With a charcoal stick, she drew Thomas True and Mrs. True. When she finished drawing Josiah, she said, "Now you can come and watch me paint."

For the next of many days the art maker painted, and Josiah paid close attention.

She squeezed paint from the leather pouches onto her palette. She chose her brushes carefully.

Patience Cage had looked at Thomas True and had seen a kind man with soft blue eyes and a fine nose. That was how she painted him. She looked at Mrs. True and saw a dark-eyed lady with a hidden smile and small hands. That was how she painted her. She looked at Josiah and painted a friend.

Then one day she was finished. Patience Cage picked up a very small bristled brush. Along the rim of a goldfish bowl that everyone imagined might sit on the red milk-painted table near the white settee, she signed her name like this:

By P. Cage—September 10, 1817.

P.Cage - 1817

The True family hung their portrait in the small room with the white settee between the two windows.

At last Patience Cage was ready to continue her traveling. She took up her cloak, and from its folds pressed something into Josiah's hand.

"I know that one day you will use this," she said.

Josiah looked down to see the small brush, its bristles bound in a way never to come undone.

"I will," he promised the art maker. "I will."

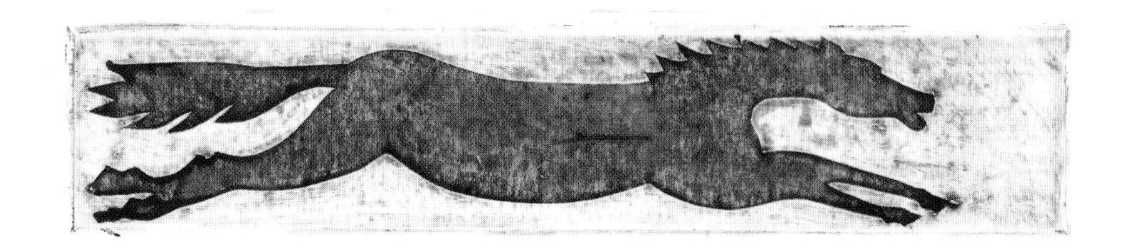

Years would pass and Josiah would leave his father's farm to go west, up the Missouri River. He would carry a palette and easel and paint the portraits of Kansas warriors against the broad flatland, free of trees and hills.

And when he heard them say, "Why, he can see into the very soul of a man!" Josiah knew that he had kept his promise to the art maker.